SUNNY DAYS

WITH
MOMMY & ME

WRITTEN BY JENNIFER ROSARIO DE CASIANO

ILLUSTRATED BY MEGAN LAWSON

EAST 26TH
PUBLISHING

For permissions requests, contact the publisher at www.east26thpublishing.com

Library of Congress Cataloging-in-Publication data is available
ISBN: (Hardback) 978-1-955077-40-8 | (Paperback) 978-1-955077-41-5 |
(eBook) 978-1-955077-42-2

10 9 8 7 6 5 4 3 2 1
First printing edition 2021

East 26th Publishing
Houston, TX

DEDICATED TO...

Above all, to God, as a thank offering.
It was through Him
that I found strength, hope and joy
in raising my son as a single mother.

To Marcos, for being such an amazingly pleasant and joyful kid.
I am extremely blessed and proud to call you my son.

To my own Mom, Dad & family, who were, undoubtedly, my "village."
Thank you for the roles you played in helping make this a true story.
Your stories are coming next!

To my husband, whom I now share my life with;
thank you for your encouragement and loving support in writing my story.

And to all of you single parents out in the world;
stay strong, seek the Lord and may you find joy on your journey as a parent.
You can do this!

"For I know the plans I have for you, declares the Lord,
plans to prosper you and not to harm you, plans to give you hope and a future."
Jeremiah 29:11

Love, Jenny

Glory be to God!
Psalm 63:3-5

Mommy and I live alone with our dog, Harley.
Even though our family is small, and life is not always perfect,
my Mommy teaches me how to enjoy each day to the fullest.

Mommy knows that I don't quite understand time yet,
but she knows that I understand the order in which we do things.

She says this is called a routine.

I love our routine because I always know what happens next.
That makes me feel confident and helps me know what I'm supposed to do.

I love spending time with my mommy.

We learn important lessons together every day.

Mommy wakes me every morning with lots of kisses and says,
"It's time to rise and shine!"
She always calls me her little sunshine.

Everyone needs sunshine.
God tells us to be a light in the world, so that's what we try to do.

Mommy makes me a healthy breakfast every morning.

She says it's the most important meal of the day because it gives my body energy and my brain thinking power.

My favorite breakfast is waffles with LOTS of berries.

She makes my waffles look like the sun.
I love dipping them into my sweet maple syrup. Yum!

After breakfast, she rides me to school on her bicycle.
Her bicycle pulls a little wagon in the back called a rickshaw.

I get to sit in there reading my books.
I even get to look out of the little window and watch things go by.

It's so much fun.
Mommy says she likes the exercise and the cool breeze on her face.

She walks me into school, where I have a fun day...

learning from my teachers ...

and playing with my friends.

Today I made a fun finger painting
with my eyes closed, while listening to music.

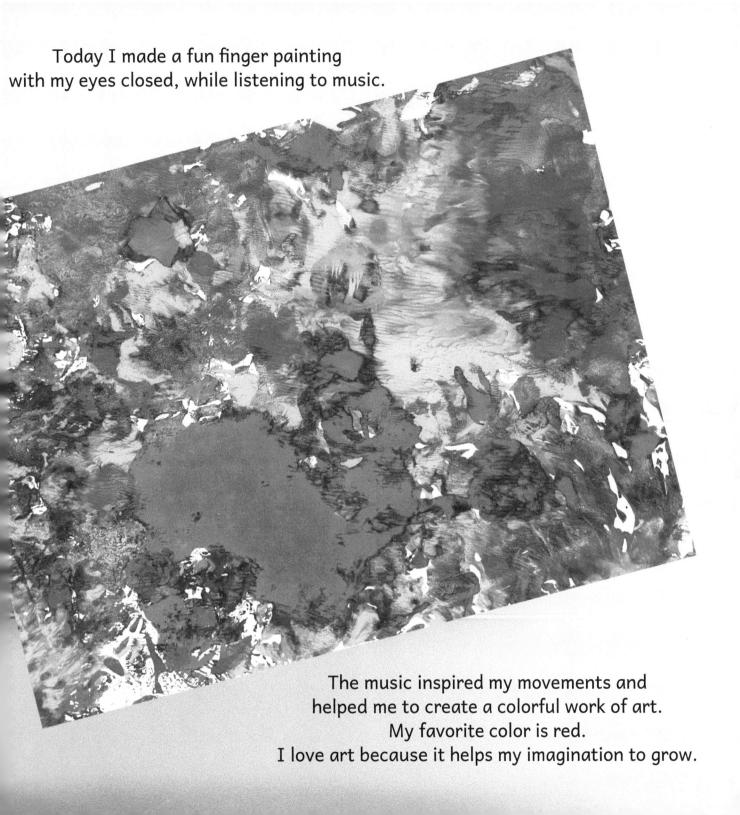

The music inspired my movements and
helped me to create a colorful work of art.
My favorite color is red.
I love art because it helps my imagination to grow.

When I'm at school, mommy works.

Sometimes she works at home,

and sometimes she gets to work in front of a camera!

On the days she doesn't pick me up from school on her bike,
we ride in Mommy's car.

I like taking rides in her car because I get to tell her about everything
that I did that day, and she tells me about what she did at work.

We also like to sing songs together.

She laughs at me because I always take my shoes and socks off in the car.
It just feels so good to wiggle my toes!

After we get home, we have a little rest time before homework.

Sometimes we watch my favorite animal shows.
I love to learn interesting facts about all the different animals.

Other days we play soccer with my puppy outside.
Mommy says it's important to exercise our bodies to keep them strong.

One time, we grew a butterfly garden and released the butterflies after school!

We started with baby caterpillars and fed them nectar each day.

We watched them grow until they turned into cocoons and took careful notes of the changes we observed.

Then, one day, the butterflies emerged from their cocoons
and flew around inside of their habitat.

The caterpillars' transformation into butterflies is called "metamorphosis."

Mommy and I took the butterflies outside and released them in our front yard.

he says that butterflies are a symbol of hope
nd that we should always have hope and faith
n our hearts.

When I think of hope, it reminds me of my daddy.
I don't get to see him much, which makes me sad.

My daddy is in the military and helps to protect our country.
I miss him and worry about him.

Sometimes, I have troubl
remembering him,
so mommy helps me by
showing me pictures and
videos, and telling me
stories about things we'v
done together.

She also helps me write him letters.
Each day she reminds me how much he loves me.

We don't need to be together every day
to feel each other's love.

Then, it's time for mommy to cook dinner.
I like doing my homework in the kitchen close to her
so she can help me when I have questions.
She's super smart and always checks my homework
to make sure I understand what I'm learning.

We always eat together at the dinner table.

Dinner is a fun time for me because we get to tell each other stories.
I tell mommy about the new things I'm learning at school,
and she tells me about daddy's adventures.

Today I will surprise her with the painting I made at school.

Mommy says eating together is important quality time.

On treat nights, she gives me dessert like a fruit salad or ice cream after dinner.
Mmm, fruit salad is so good!

After dinner, I rush to practice my piano lessons on my own.
I really love music.
t's fun to play, it helps me to focus, and it brings so much joy to others.
I'm happy to be a musician and can't wait to keep learning.

Then,
sometimes we play a board game together...

Or I play with my toys
by myself for a little while.

I like to imagine what my daddy
is doing as a soldier and I pretend
that my animals are helping him to
protect people all around the world.

So, I line them up and prepare
them for battle like superheroes.

After play time is over,
I clean up and put my toys away.

Mommy gives me stars for doing my chores.

I get to earn rewards with the stars.

But I know that helping Mommy around the house is really important because she works hard, takes care of me, and does so many chores around the house all by herself.

She gets tired after a long day, so it feels good to help mommy when I can.

I know it makes her happy too.
We make a good team!

And, of course, before bedtime, it's bath time!
I also brush my teeth.
Staying clean is important for our health and feels so good.
But I mostly enjoy pretending that my bath toys are having a pool party.

Splish splash!

After my bath, we mark off another day on my calendar.
Today was one of my best days! I did so many things I enjoy:
I learned new things, I played with my friends, I ate well, I played music,
and best of all, I spent time with my mommy.

Next is a bedtime story.
Mommy loves reading to me, but now I enjoy reading to her.
I love reading books about travel adventures.
It helps me learn about all the different states and countries.
One day I will get to travel all around the world and tell my own stories.

Tickle Time!
I ask mommy to tickle me before bed.
I love to laugh until my belly aches.
It's so much fun!

The very last thing we do before I go to sleep is pray.

Praying allows us to talk to God and tell Him how grateful
we are for all the wonderful blessings in our lives.

We can also ask Him to help us with anything we are struggling with.

Thank you, Lord, for a fun day!
Thank you for my mommy, my daddy, my family, my school,
my friends, my home, my food, my puppy and my warm bed.

Please bless my mommy and me again tomorrow and every day.
And please protect my daddy.

Oh, and please bless all the world with good families,
good homes, yummy food, warm beds and lots of love.

I love you. Amen!

Good night!

Jenny and her son, Marcos

Author Jennifer Rosario de Casiano

is an actor, spokesperson, author, and philanthropist living in Florida with her husband. Jenny wrote this book based on her own experience as a single mother to her son, Marcos. She has significantly fond memories of their time together living with their dog, Harley, when Marcos was between four and six years old. Marcos now attends Yale University while Jenny writes children's books, continues to work as an actor and enjoys taking part in missionary work around the world.

CPSIA information can be obtained
at www.ICGtesting.com
Printed in the USA
BVHW020845161121
621686BV00005BA/225